Keeping Silkworms

Josephine Croser

Contents

Introduction

This book is about looking after silkworms. It tells you how to collect their silk and use it.

Setting up the Farm

To set up a farm you will need:

- about 30 silkmoth eggs
- a few cardboard boxes
- fresh mulberry leaves
- a soft paintbrush
- cardboard
- scissors
- a small comb

Put the silkmoth eggs into a box and place it in a room with fresh air and light.

Warning!

Don't put silkworms, moths or eggs:

- in direct sunlight;
- near a heater;
- under an airconditioner;
- where insect spray may drift onto them.

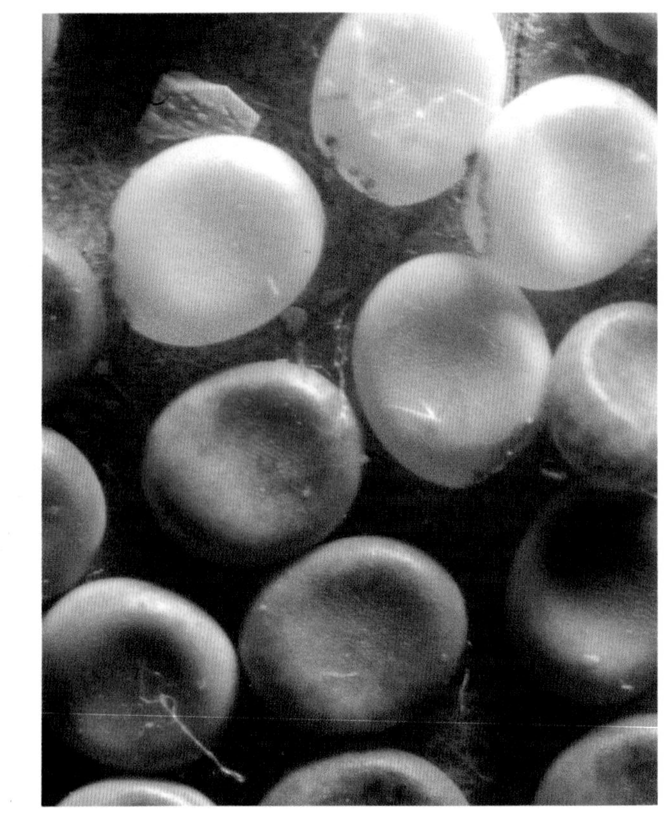

Silkmoth eggs magnified

Caring for Silkworms

Your silkmoth eggs will hatch in Spring. Silkworms eat mulberry leaves. When they begin to hatch, put in a fresh mulberry leaf. After the silkworms have crawled onto it, put the leaf into another box. This stops the silkworms from crawling over the new ones which are trying to hatch. Do this each day until hatching has ended.

A newly-hatched silkworm

Pick fresh mulberry leaves each day or store some in a plastic bag in a refrigerator.

For the first two weeks, feed your silkworms three times a day. Make sure you only give them small leaves. Dry the leaves if they are wet.

Use a soft paintbrush to lift the silkworms onto new leaves. Check both sides of each old leaf to make sure there are no silk-worms left on it. Then throw the old leaves away.

Choosing mulberry leaves

Brushing silkworms onto fresh leaf

When they are two or three weeks old, the silkworms move quickly from old leaves to new ones without help. Now feed them larger leaves and feed them more often.

You also need some extra boxes. Put about five or six silkworms into each box so they are not overcrowded. Empty their droppings from the boxes each day.

Overcrowded silkworms

Separating silkworms into boxes

Observing Silkworms Moulting

Silkworms go through changes before they are ready to spin. As they grow, silkworms get too big for their skins, so they shed the old ones. This is called *moulting*. It usually takes one day.

When silkworms are about to moult, they stop eating and hold their heads high, until they get rid of the old skin. They moult at about 6 days, 12 days, 18 days and 26 days. Silkworms moult four times before they are ready to spin.

A silkworm next to its old skin

Observing Silkworms Spinning

Silkworms usually begin to spin when they are five to six weeks old. Some may spin even earlier. You can tell when silkworms are about to spin because they:

- stop eating;
- become shorter;
- wave their heads in the air;
- lose a drop of brownish liquid from their mouths.

At this time you separate the silkworms so their silk does not tangle as they spin. Divide a clean box with cardboard pieces. Put each silkworm into its own space.

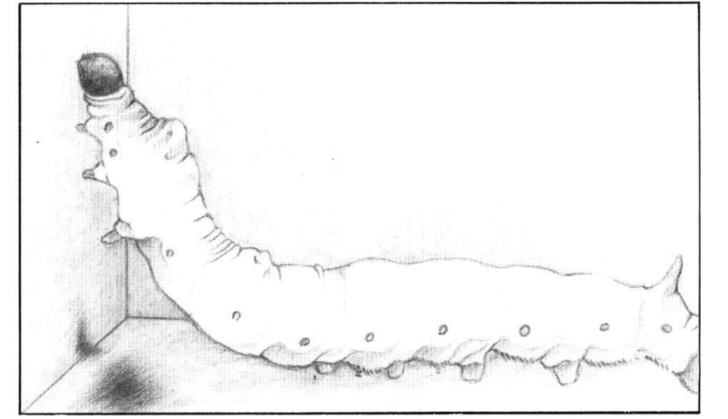

Silkworm ready to spin

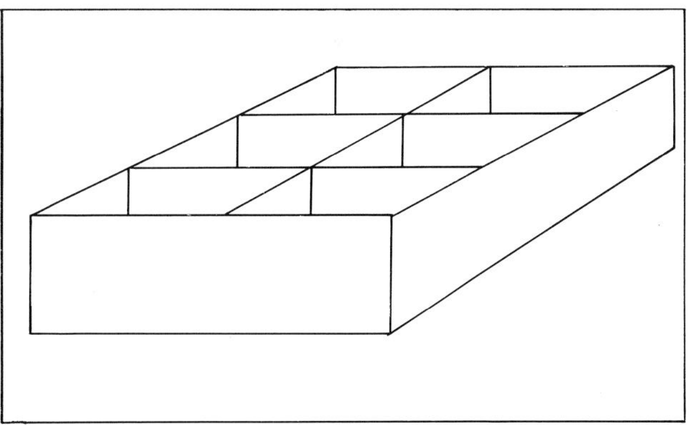

Box with cardboard dividers

Look for these changes when your silkworm spins its cocoon.

1. The silkworm attaches itself to the box.

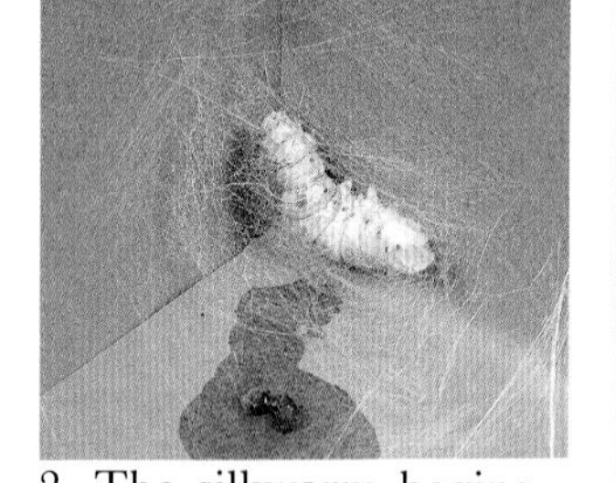

2. The silkworm begins its cocoon. It is made of one long thread.

3. The cocoon after 14 hours of spinning

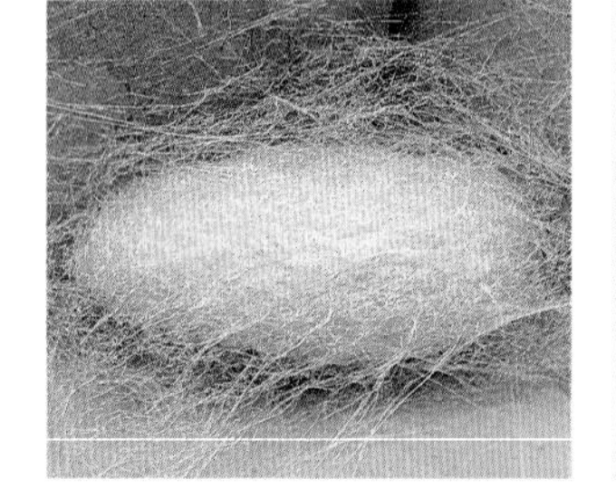

4. The cocoon after 24 hours. Inside, the silkworm keeps spinning for 48–72 hours.

5. During the next 2–3 days, inside the cocoon, the silkworm changes into a pupa. The cocoon has been cut to show the pupa.

Collecting the Silk

You can collect the silk one week after the spinning begins, by winding it onto a piece of cardboard. (See steps 1 to 6.) Put each pupa back into a box. Keep a few cocoons to observe later.

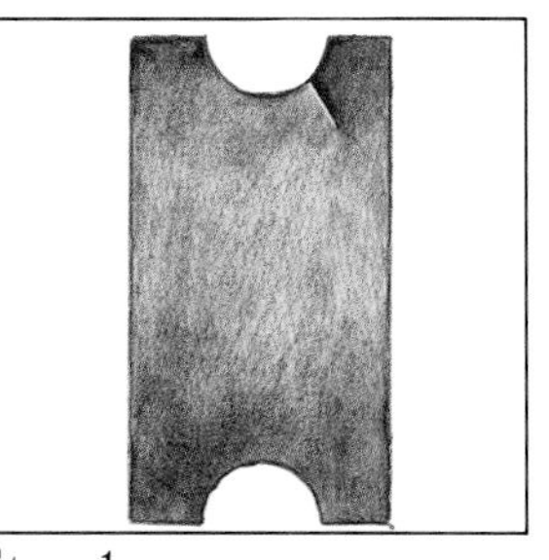

Step 1.
Make a cardboard winder. (See back cover.)

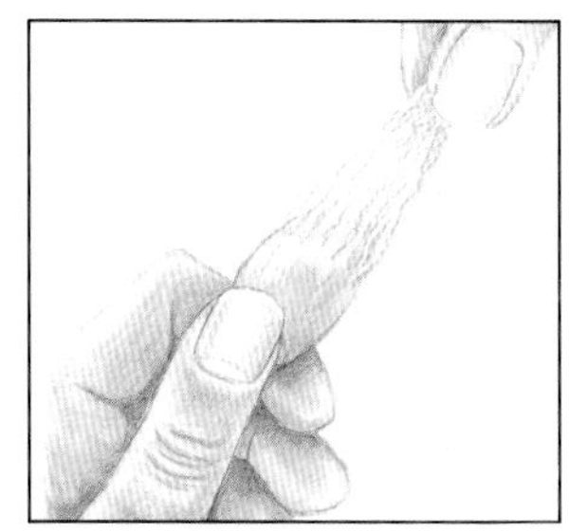

Step 2.
Carefully pull the outside threads to one end of the cocoon.

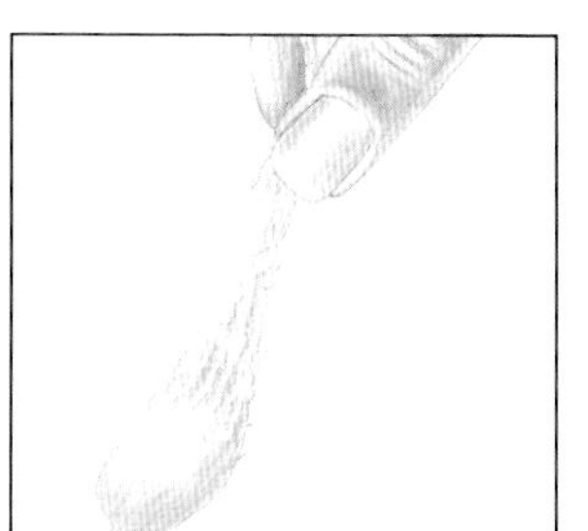

Step 3.
Hold these threads, let the cocoon dangle, and shake it gently up and down.

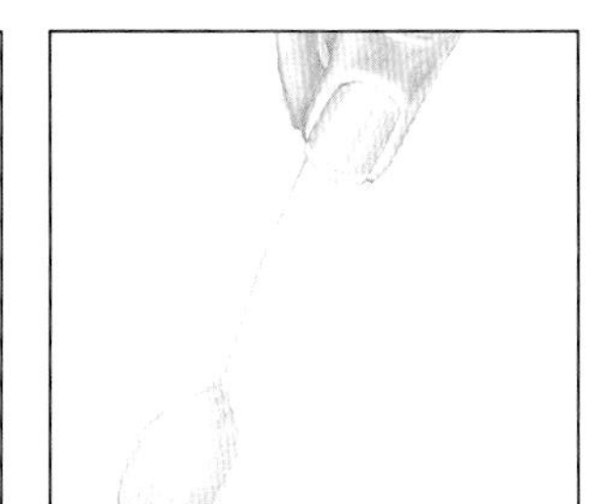

Step 4.
Repeat steps 2. and 3. until you have one thread.

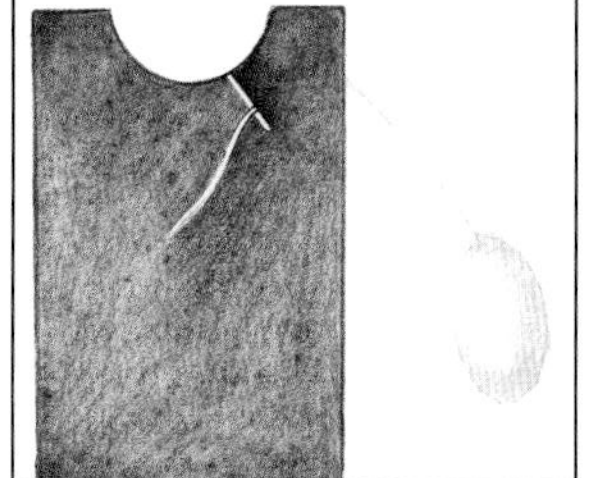

Step 5.
Slip the thread into the slit in the winder.

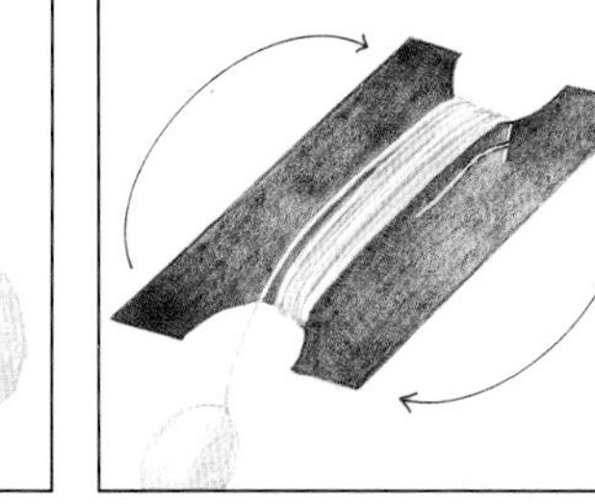

Step 6.
Turn the winder over and over.

Using the Silk

One way of using the silk is to make a bookmark.

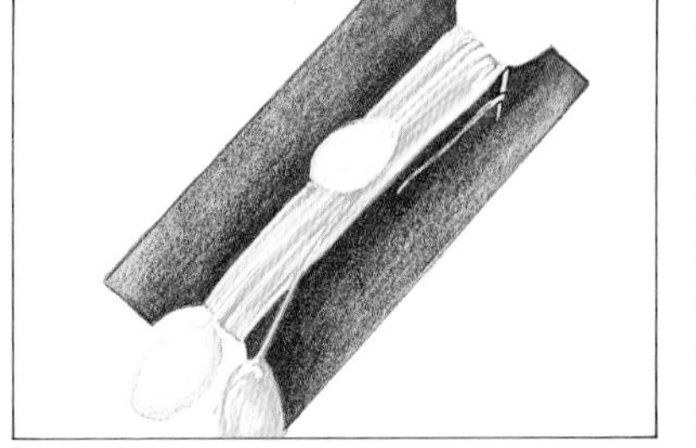

Step 1.
Wind the silk from three cocoons onto your winder.

Step 2.
Cut the silk to remove it.

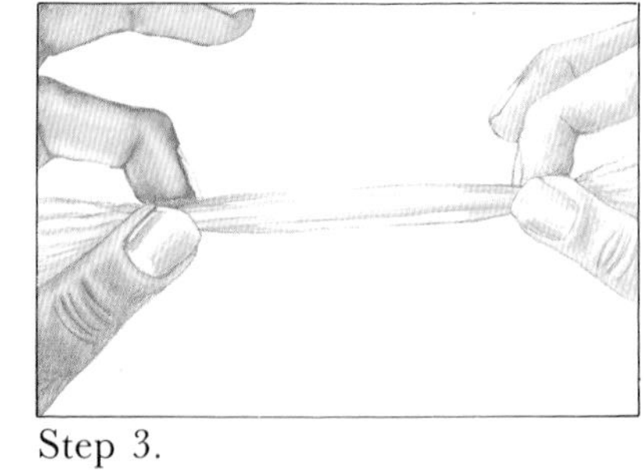

Step 3.
Find a partner to help you.
Take one end of the silk each.

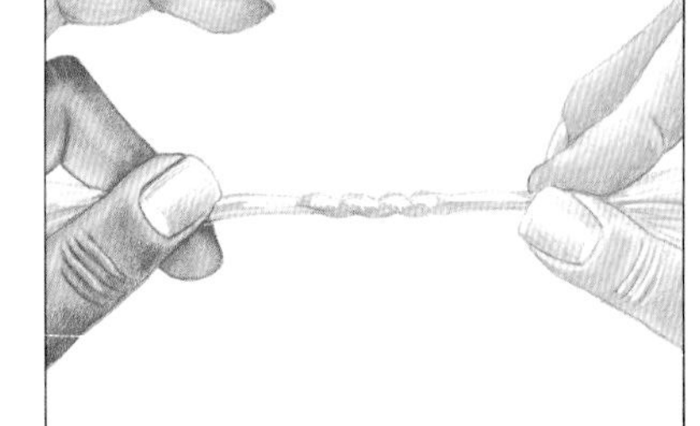

Step 4.
Twist it in opposite directions.

Step 5.
Take the silk from your partner.
Hold it in a firm, straight line.

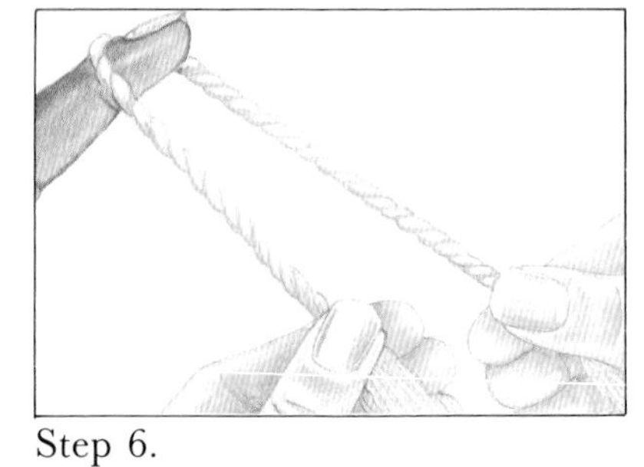

Step 6.
Fold it in halves around your partner's finger.

Step 7.
Hold both ends in one hand.

Step 8.
Squeeze the halves together with your other hand.

Step 9.
Lift the loop off your partner's finger. Pull it quickly between your finger and thumb.

Step 10.
Tie the loose ends.

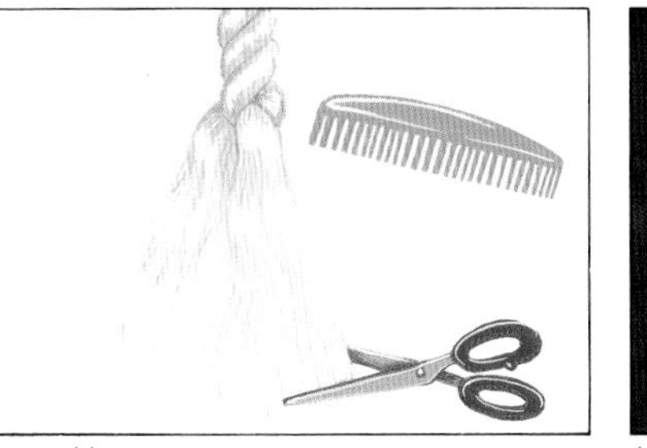

Step 11.
Comb the ends and snip any untidy thread.

A finished bookmark

Preparing for the Next Season

Two or three weeks after spinning, moths will come out of the cocoons and pupae. Put male and female moths into the same box so they can mate. The females' eggs will then be fertile and will hatch next year.

Male silkmoth

Silkmoth with its empty cocoon

Female silkmoth laying egg

The females have large bodies. They are packed with eggs. Their feelers are slightly feathery.

The males have thinner bodies. Their feelers are very feathery.

The moths do not need food or drink, and they do not fly. After mating, the female lays hundreds of eggs. In a few days the moths die. Collect all the eggs and put them in a cool, dry place. They will begin to hatch in spring.

Male and female silkmoths mating

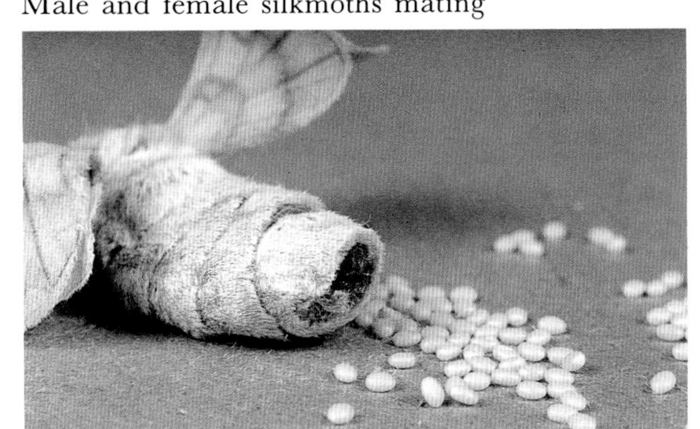

Female silkmoth and eggs

Time Line – Seasons

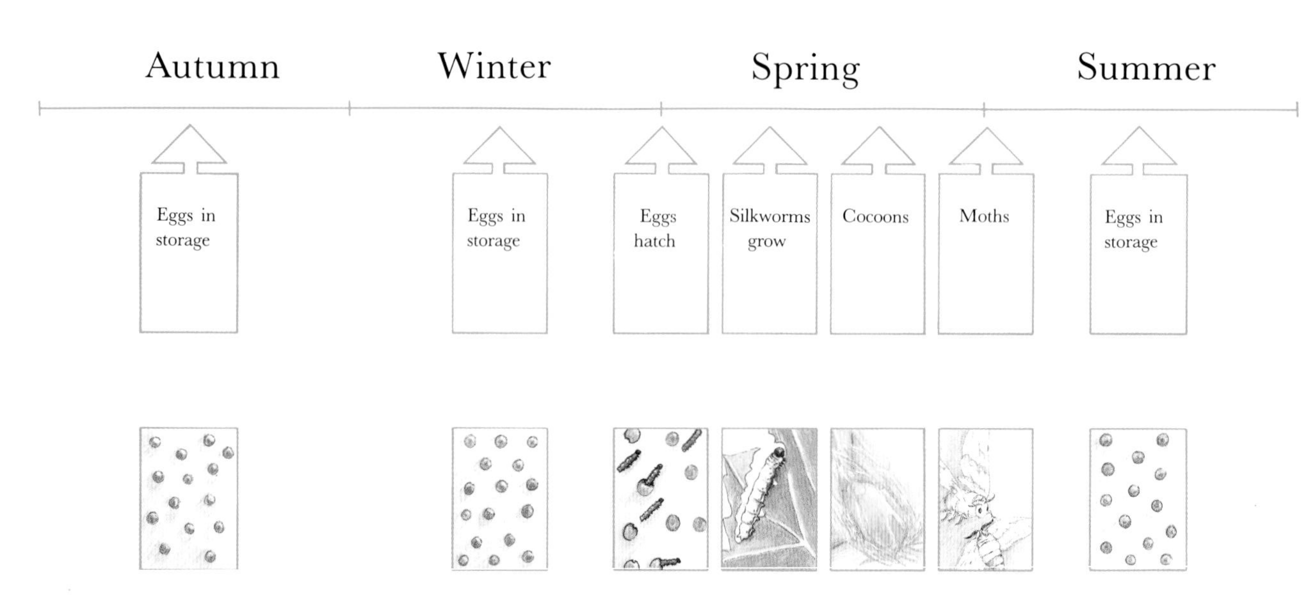

These are approximate times only. Your silkworms may take more or less time to go through these changes.

Time Line – Weeks

Life Cycle of a Silkworm

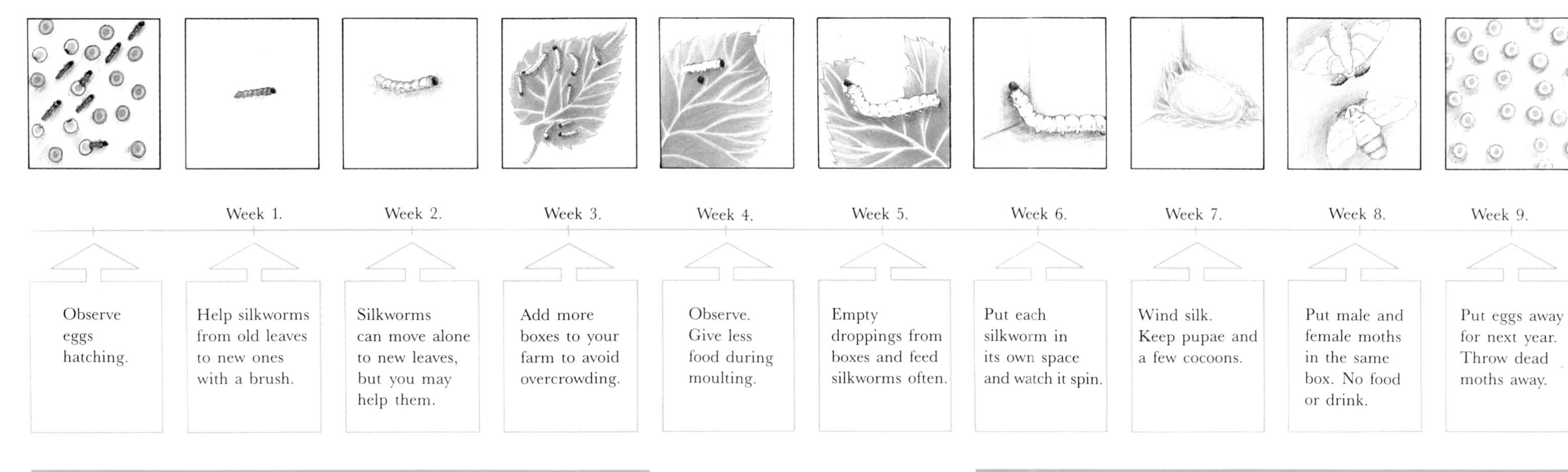

What You Need to Do

These are approximate times only. Your silkworms may take more or less time to go through these changes.

Index

Further References

Silkworms, Densey Clyne
(Angus and Robertson, 1984)

Silkworms, Sylvia Johnson and Isao Kishida (A Lerner Natural Science Book, 1982)

A silkworm is born, Ann Stepp
(Oak Tree Press Co, 1973)

The silkworm story, Oxford Scientific Films (André Deutsch Ltd, London, 1983)

Where to get Silkmoth Eggs

- Schools
- Local natural history museums
- The "wanted to buy or sell" section of local newspapers
- Nature resource centres for schools